This Walker book

belongs to:

- - - - - - - - -

- - - - - - - - -

For Dorothy,

with lots of love from Gumble. x

V. F.

For Patsy, Amelia, Cora, Catnip

and Dexter the dog.

With lots of thanks to Reception class,

Great Tew School.

S. H.

First published 2010 by Walker Books Ltd

87 Vauxhall Walk, London SE11 5HJ

This edition published 2010

4 6 8 10 9 7 5 3

Text © 2010 Vivian French
Illustrations © 2010 Sue Heap

This book has been typeset in Carnation

Printed in China

British Library Cataloguing in Publication Data:
a catalogue record for this book is available from the British Library

ISBN 978-1-4063-2738-0

www.walker.co.uk

WALKER BOOKS

AND SUBSIDIARIES

LONDON · BOSTON · SYDNEY · AUCKLAND

Polly's Pink Pyjamas

Vivian French   Sue Heap

Polly loved her pink pyjamas.

What did she wear
when she went
to bed?

PINK PYJAMAS!

What did she wear
when she got up?

PINK PYJAMAS!

What did she wear
when she ate her
breakfast?

PINK PYJAMAS!

What did Polly wear ALL DAY LONG?

PINK PYJAMAS!

Then, one Monday morning,
RAT-A-TAT-TAT!

Polly ran to open
the front door.

"Hello, Polly!" said Fred.

"Will you come to my party?"

"Yes, please," said Polly. "I LOVE parties!"

"Good!" said Fred. "Come round to my house at five o'clock."

Polly

And off he ran.

"Oh," said Polly.
"What shall I wear?

I need ...

a DRESS, a CARDIGAN,
SOCKS and SHOES.

I know! I'll go and see Mia."

Polly ran to Mia's house.

"Hello, Mia, I need a dress!"

"You can have my red spotty dress," said Mia.

"Thank you,"
said Polly, and she
put on the dress.

"And now I'll go and see Jo."

Polly hurried to Jo's house.

"Jo! Jo! I need a cardigan!"

"You can have my green check cardigan," said Jo.

"Thank you,"
said Polly, and she
put on the cardigan.

♥ ♥ ♥

"And now I'll go and see Harry."

Polly rushed to Harry's house.

"Hello, Harry, I need some socks!"

"You can borrow my stripy socks," said Harry.

"Thank you,"
said Polly,
and she pulled on the socks.

"One last thing," Polly told herself.

"I'll go and see Claire."

Polly rushed to Claire's house.

"Claire! Claire! I need some shoes!"
"You can have my blue
shiny shoes," said Claire.

"Thank you,"
said Polly, and she
put on the shoes.

"Thank you very much INDEED!"

Polly went home.

"Now I'm ready for the party!" she said.

She went to look in the mirror —

and she stared and she stared

and she stared.

The red spotty dress

was MUCH too SHORT.

The green check cardigan

was MUCH too SMALL.

The stripy socks

were MUCH too LONG.

And the blue shiny shoes

were MUCH too BIG.

"Oh, NO!" said Polly.

And she cried and she cried
and she cried.

Until...

Ting-a-ling! Ting-a-ling!

The phone rang.

Polly answered it.

"Polly," said Fred. "Why aren't you at my party?"

"Oh, Fred!" sobbed Polly. "I can't come to your party!
I've got no party clothes and no party shoes!"

"But, Polly," said Fred, "it's not a party clothes party.
It's a SPECIAL party.
We're going to have PIZZA.
We're going to have HOT CHOCOLATE.
Dad's reading us
BEDTIME
STORIES...

It's a PYJAMA party!"

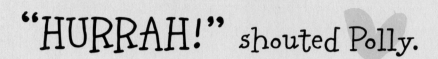

"HURRAH!" shouted Polly.

"Hurrah hurrah
   HURRAH!!!

I'll be there
in just a minute!"

And Polly took off ...

the blue shiny shoes,

the stripy socks,

the green check cardigan

and the red spotty dress.

And what do you think
Polly wore to Fred's party?

PINK PYJAMAS!!!!

Also by Vivian French

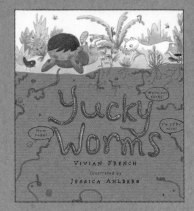

ISBN 978-1-4063-1458-8

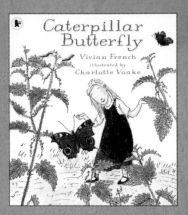

ISBN 978-1-4063-1277-5

Other books by Sue Heap

ISBN 978-1-4063-2333-1

ISBN 978-1-4063-2597-3

Available from all good book stores

www.walker.co.uk